The Vicwelt Mansion

Story and Art by:
John Wayne Greene III

Special thanks to my family and friends for all of their help and support. Special Thanks to God for giving me such a supportive family and the talent to bring you this great story.

This story contains scenes of brief nudity and brief profanity. The characters and events in this story are entirely fictional. Any resemblance to real people and real events is entirely coincidental.

ISBN 978-1-105-05023-7

Copyright © 2011 by John Wayne Greene III

Table of Contents

Chapter 1

It was 11:32pm on a Friday night in the town of Vicwelt. A car with a brightly lit sign that said Velo Nacho's Pizza was driving down a forest road.

"I can't believe this place is apart of our delivery area." said the woman driving the car.

She is a twenty-two year old Caucasian woman with her long black hair in a ponytail. She was wearing the blue and purple Velo Nacho cap and uniform. This was the last delivery of her first day as a pizza delivery woman.

"Why did I take this job anyway?" thought the woman.

One week ago, she walked off the stage at the Ten Pleasures Strip club. She had only started working there three months ago to help pay for her college classes. She quickly became popular among the regular customers. However they quickly got tired of her act. As a result the club's officials wanted her to perform some extreme things on stage to get the customers even more interested. She didn't want to do those things and left the stage as soon as it was announced to the audience that she was about to perform them.

Soon after a brief argument with the club's staff, she found herself sitting alone at a bus stop down the street waiting for the bus. It was in the middle of the night and all she had on was her overcoat that was covering the dark blue leather lingerie she was wearing. Suddenly a car drove up to the bus stop. She recognized the man in the car as one of the regular customers at the club.

"Forget it! I'm not some cheap whore. I'm just going home." She said.

"I wasn't going to ask that Pepper. I just wanted to see if you would like a ride home. I heard all of that fussing going on backstage." said the man.

"You and everyone else heard it. I'm not going back there. I guess I'll take your offer." She said as she got in the car.

"So you're not going to dance anymore, Pepper?" asked the man as he drove the car.

"Please don't call me by that nickname. My name is Kimberly. I guess I'll have to find work elsewhere." said Kimberly.

"Kimberly that is a nice name, my name is Bill. I own a pizza shop. Have you ever ordered from Velo Nacho's Pizza before?" asked Bill.

"Yeah, I ordered… HUH! You own the place!" said a surprised Kimberly.

Bill laughed a little at her response.

"Yup, The shop is about to have its 5th anniversary, but we're short on delivery personnel. If you want I'll hire you. The job doesn't pay like a stripper's income, but it can help until you find something else." said Bill.

"I'll think about it." said Kimberly.

They soon arrived at the apartment complex where Kimberly lived. Bill took her up to the front of her apartment building before they parted ways. Once inside of her apartment she took off her overcoat and tossed it on her couch. Kimberly sat down at her desk and looked over her college papers to try and forget about tonight's earlier events. She was studying to be a video game designer. Beside the papers were a few game demos she made. Looking at them made her realize one thing. She needed money.

A few days later Kimberly walked into the Velo Nacho's pizza shop and was hired. Kimberly's job was simple when she wasn't delivering any orders she would help keep the shop clean. When it was getting near closing time Kimberly entered the shop after delivering three pizza party packs to some kid's late night party. As Kimberly handed over the cash from the delivery Bill came up to her carrying a pizza box.

"This is the last order for today. It is for the mansion on the hillside of town." said Bill.

"We delivery all the way out there, isn't that area mostly nothing but forest?" asked Kimberly as she took the pizza box.

"Well it is just twenty minutes away by car so it's no problem. Also I would like for you to try these. It's my new pizza sticks recipe. Tell me what you think of them when you get back." said Bill as he gave her a small cardboard box.

"Sure." said Kimberly as she left back out.

It was now 11:40pm as Kimberly reached the address. However there was a fancy eight foot tall iron gate that blocked her from going up to the mansion. The sculptured pattern on the gates looked European and there were two tiny mermaid statues at the top of the gate. Kimberly picked up her cell phone and dialed the mansion's number.

"Hello, I'm here with the order for Mr. Rowich. Can you please open the gate?" asked Kimberly.

"Very well." said a man over the phone before he hung up.

Kimberly saw the gates slowly open. As the gates opened they made a creaking sound as if they hadn't been opened in months. While she drove the car into the mansion's estate she saw how big the yard was. It looked like it was recently cut and was as long as two football fields. While driving up the pathway she took out one of the pizza sticks Bill asked her to try out and ate it.

"Bill, too much of a spicy aftertaste." thought Kimberly.

A few seconds later she reached the mansion. It was a European style mansion and it was three stories tall. The lights were on in some of the rooms which made the gold curtains in the windows glow brightly.

Kim got out of the car with a pizza box and walked up the steps to the front door. Before she could knock the mansion's owner opened the door. He opened the door so fast it made Kimberly's heart jump. He was a middle aged man wearing a black suit and tie. He saw the startled look on Kimberly's face.

"Sorry, I didn't mean to scare you." said Mr. Rowich.

"It's okay. Here is your order. That will be $15.82" said Kimberly as she handed him the pizza box.

"Young Lady it's a long drive back to town. Would you like to stay for a bit and relax? I'll give you an extra tip if you do." said Mr. Rowich as he handed Kimberly the money.

"Oh, um, I can't I'm still on my work shift." said Kimberly as she was surprised by what he offered.

"Very well." said Mr. Rowich as he went back inside closing the door.

Kimberly quickly went back to the car. Thoughts raced in her head about what he said, a TIP just for RELAXING. She figured she was overreacting and decided to forget about it. As she drove down the long pathway she noticed something she didn't see before. The grass appeared to be taller and taller the more she drove from the mansion. Soon full grown weeds were in her sights, it was as if the grass was never cut.

"That's strange, well maybe I missed it when coming up." said Kimberly as she thought nothing of it.

That was until she saw the gate again. It was closed. But more so, it had changed it was now seventeen feet tall. The gate no longer looked fancy but now rundown and rusted. The two tiny mermaid statues that were at the top of the gate were now replaced by small statues of bird skeletons. Curious and confused about her surroundings she got out of the car.

"I must have gone the wrong way, wait the road is just one way, but there is no way that this is the same gate." said Kimberly as she looked over the area.

She took out her cell phone and tried calling the mansion's number but the battery in her phone suddenly died.

"Just great, I'll have to drive back to tell them to open the gate." said Kimberly.

Kimberly got back in the car. Her eyes opened wide in disbelief as the car wouldn't start up. She tried to start it up another three times with no success. Kimberly left the car by the gate and started walking back up the long pathway.

"Why is this happening? I hope that old man doesn't get the wrong idea but I have to use his phone to call my boss." thought Kimberly.

As Kimberly walked she got a closer look at the tall grass and weeds. There appeared to be no cut grass anywhere now. Kimberly couldn't believe that the grass had suddenly grown. She reached down to break off a blade of grass then the loud sound of a dog's aggressive barking was heard. Startled by this Kimberly tripped and fell. She then heard the sound of frantic rustling from the tall grass behind her.

"EEPP!" screamed Kimberly as she turned around just in time to see three cats jump out of the grass onto her.

The cats quickly ran back into the grass on the other side of the yard. Kimberly stood back up. The cats give her such a fright that she was catching her breath and had her hand over her heart. They had to be running from the dog she heard so Kimberly braced herself for a dog attack. However after about a minute or two the only thing she heard was just the wind. Kimberly decided to speed walk up to the mansion.

"Come on! This has got to be some type of joke." said Kimberly as she saw the mansion.

Just like the gate the mansion looked rundown almost as if people abandoned it over a hundred years ago. There were now weeds and trees tangled and growing against the east and west walls of the mansion. No lights were on in the mansion. The glass windows were all broken as if someone had thrown rocks at them. The curtains in the windows weren't gold but dirty brown and ripped. Kimberly saw someone quickly peak out one of the second floor windows. It was too dark to fully see their face. Soon Kimberly made it to the mansion's front steps.

"This is crazy. It wasn't like this before." said Kimberly as she saw the steps cracked in many places with weeds growing out of them.

Kimberly walked up the steps. When she touched the third step part of it broke off. Kimberly caught her balance so she wouldn't fall. She stopped and just looked around again. She couldn't believe anything she was seeing. It was as if the area had aged many years in just a few minutes. However, for now the most important thing to her was to get them to open the gate and have the car towed.

"Hello." said Kimberly as she knocked on the front door.

She waited a bit, but there was no answer, so she knocked again. She knocked a few more times and still there was no response from the other side. In her impatience, almost by reflex, she put her hand on the door knob and turned it. She was a little shocked to see that the door was unlocked. As Kimberly entered into the mansion's lobby area a few dim lights turned on barely lighting up the room.

"Hello? Mr. Rowich?" said Kimberly, but then she felt a really cold breeze hit her back.

Kimberly turned around to close the door but the door was gone. It was as if the door was never there. She quickly felt the wall around the area where the door was.

"This isn't happening... This isn't happening!" said Kimberly as all she felt was the smooth sheetrock the wall was made out of.

Suddenly the floor started to rumble. Kimberly backed up, as she saw an unbelievable sight. Starting at the wall where the door was the floor was breaking apart. It wasn't a basement that the floor was falling into, but what appeared to be a dark black void. Kimberly quickly looked around for a way out. There were no windows to climb out of, but there was a doorway on the other side of the lobby. Kimberly ran for it, and soon found herself in a hallway.

"Shit!" said Kimberly as she heard the sound of the crumbling floor coming closer.

Kimberly ran down the hallway, but briefly looked back. The floor was falling apart faster then before. However, the part of the hallway that was on the other side of the doorway she entered was untouched. It was as if the crumbling floor was following her! The crumbling floor was now just inches from her feet. She saw a set of stairs just up ahead leading to the second floor. Feeling the floor under her about to collapse, Kimberly did a big leap onto the steps. She ran up the steps as fast as she could. Once Kimberly reached the second floor hallway she stopped to quickly catch her breath.

"This is nuts! Huh..." said Kimberly as she no longer heard the sound of the floor falling apart.

Kimberly turned around to look at the steps but as she did a giant stone hand came out of the wall and slapped her whole body! She was sent rolling a few feet down the hallway.

"OWWW!" yelled Kimberly as she sat up.

Suddenly her screams of pain turned into a stunned silence, as she now saw eight huge stone hands coming out of the walls. They all joined clamping together blocking the stairs that led down to the first floor.

Chapter 2

Kimberly stood up holding her left arm, as it was hurt the most from the giant hand's attack. She wasn't sure if she should be thankful or not. Did the giant stone hands stop the floor from falling apart? Either way, it was clear that she couldn't go back down that way.

"I guess this is the bedroom area, but it looks like it hasn't been used in years." said Kimberly as she looked down the second floor hallway.

The hallway was long with eight rooms on each side. The doors were all closed. The walls have cracks in them and even a few holes showing off the inner wood construction of the walls. There were a few small tables in the hallway that had vases with dead plants on top of them. Most of the chandeliers in the hallway had broken light bulbs while a few that did have working bulbs barely lit up the hallway. Suddenly the loud sound of barking was heard again.

"What the…!" yelled Kimberly as she was startled.

Kimberly turned back around looking at the stone hands the barking was coming from behind them. In a small opening between two of the stone hands black smoke could be seen coming from it. Within the smoke two golden eyes opened wide glowing brightly. Kimberly couldn't look away from them it was as if she was being mesmerized. Her daze was broke, as a black furred paw with long black claws forced its way past the opening. She quickly ran for the first door she saw.

"Open! DARN IT OPEN!" yelled Kimberly as she tried to turn the door knob and banged on the door.

Franticly, Kimberly ran to the next door trying to open it. She started to cough as smoke filled the area. She looked at the giant hands once more. The dog, still barking, was half way out of the hand's opening. Smoke was heavily coming from its body, and its sharp fangs were tainted with smoke and blood.

"Shit! SHIT! OPEN UP!" yelled Kimberly as she started ramming and kicking the door.

"Pepper in here! Hurry!" said a man's voice.

"Roland?" said Kimberly as she looked down the hallway.

A door to a room at the end of the hallway was slightly open. Kimberly wasting no time ran for the door and entered the room quickly closing the door behind her. Kimberly's delivery uniform suddenly started glowing brightly.

"Whoa! Too bright!" yelled Kimberly as she covered her eyes.

In a bright flash her pizza delivery uniform vanished off of her body. To Kimberly it felt as if the fabric of the uniform was just a rush of wind going pass her. She felt herself rise up slightly as her tennis shoes turned into high heels. At the same time she felt her underwear change shape and the sound of cheering men.

"Pepper, Pepper, Pepper!" yelled a crowd of excited men.

"What! No way!" yelled Kimberly as she opened her eyes and saw she was in her dark blue lingerie on the stage of the Ten Pleasures strip club.

"Pepper, take it off!" yelled a man.

"Yea, show us some boobs, BOOBS!" yelled another man.

"No, no, this can't be real." said Kimberly as she became nervous taking a few steps back.

Kimberly didn't know what to think. She was just running for her life from a strange dog just a few seconds ago. Now she found herself on the stage she hated. The club looked like it usually did. The bar was overstocked with alcoholic drinks. There were men in the dinning area lustfully looking at her. The erotic dance music playing from the club's ceiling speakers filled the room. Multi-colored spotlights lit up the stage, making parts of Kimberly's dark blue lingerie look purple and green. However Kimberly didn't dance she just stood there in disbelief.

"Don't just stand there, that's not what you get paid for! NOW DANCE!" yelled an impatient Caucasian man who was sitting at a dining table close to the stage.

"No, I don't do this anymore, Roland!" yelled Kimberly.

"You don't do this anymore? We can't have that now, can we?" asked Roland as he got up from his seat.

He did a big leap into the air. His short brown hair grew out long. His arms and hands grew three times their size. The arm's mutating muscles could be seen as his dress shirt was being ripped from the rapid growth. His pants ripped as well as his legs and feet also grew three times their size. His finger and toe nails now looked like claws.

"What the hell are you?" panicked Kimberly as she tried to run off the stage.

However Kimberly fell as Roland landed on the stage with his huge feet causing the stage to shake greatly.

"Just what do you want with me? Why am I here?" yelled Kimberly.

"You will entertain us even if we have to force you!" demanded Roland as he reached to grab her with his big hands.

Kimberly rolled out of the way to dodge him. She then quickly kicked one of his claws cracking it with her left high heel. While he was stunned by the pain she got up and ran for the backstage area. As soon as she passed by the curtains that separated the stage from the backstage area a glow of light surrounded her.

"Not again!" said Kimberly closing her eyes tightly so she wouldn't be blinded.

She felt her clothing change. She opened her eyes after a few seconds and looked down at herself. She was relieved to see that she was back in her pizza delivery uniform. The cold air hit her and she looked up seeing that she was standing in a doorway looking outside. What she saw was the back parking lot of the Velo Nacho's pizza shop. The delivery car she was driving was also parked there.

"Okay..." said Kimberly as she leaned against the doorway.

She was in the backroom of the pizza shop where they kept the ingredients and other extra kitchen supplies. She looked around to see if there was anything strange. Everything looked normal, but she didn't trust it at all. Outside all she heard was the wind and the sound of cars driving by. In the next room over, she heard the voices of co-workers and customers.

"This really is crazy, but which way do I go?" thought Kimberly.

A door on the other end of the backroom opened and Bill came in carrying a bag of cheese powder.

"Kimberly, you're back great! We have an important customer out there. I need your help preparing his food." said Bill as he put the cheese powder on the shelf.

"Are you really Bill?" asked Kimberly.

"Huh, oh… That Rowich guy is weird isn't he? Things tend to happen around there sometimes." said Bill.

"What, you know what's going on? Why is all this crazy stuff happening to me?!" demanded Kimberly.

"There is no time. We have to take care of the customer first." said Bill as he grabbed Kimberly's left arm.

"OWW, Bill, don't pull my arm like that!" said Kimberly as she was forced to run with Bill toward the kitchen.

Kimberly felt her t-shirt and bra underneath her jacket becoming tight on her. She looked down and saw the zipper clip of her closed pizza delivery jacket pop off. Her cleavage was now visible as the metal teeth of her zipper started breaking.

"Bill, stop I have a problem here?" said Kimberly as she felt the fabric of her bra and t-shirt rubbing and ripping against her skin.

Bill didn't stop he just continued leading her by the arm as they ran. Suddenly Kimberly's zipper fully broke open. Her breast busted out of her jacket exposed and expanding. Kimberly felt greatly embarrassed, her breast bounced back and forth as she was forced to run. However it was as if Bill and the other co-workers they passed by didn't even notice.

"Crap, I can't pull my arm free of him." thought Kimberly as she tried to get loose from his grip.

Kimberly's C-cup breast had swelled to the size of an H-cup by the time they rushed into the kitchen and they were still growing. Bill let go of Kimberly and she stumbled a bit but caught herself by landing in a chair. Bill walked over to the counter looking over kitchen utensils.

"Bill, I don't care about the customer! If you know something about this help me here!" yelled Kimberly.

"How shameful Kimberly. The customer comes first, always." said Bill as he finally turned around and looked at her.

"Now do you see what I was trying to…" said Kimberly as she felt something push the chair forward.

The chair was pushed up to a table causing her now jumbo sized breast to rest on it.

"At least you brought the main ingredient for his food." said Bill as he swung a butcher knife down toward her breast.

"WHOA!!" yelled Kimberly as she pushed the chair back quickly avoiding the knife by less then an inch.

This caused her to fall out of the chair and she hit the floor face first. Kimberly quickly stood up on her feet and was about to run, but then saw she was now alone in a different room. There wasn't even a flash of light this time. She looked down at her breast. They were back to normal size and her uniform's jacket was zipped back up. She quickly turned her head looking left and right in the room. It was an abandoned bedroom.

"I have to get out of here or I'm going to go nuts." said Kimberly as she walked over to a window and saw the mansion's front yard down below.

Looking down at the yard she wondered if she really left the room or was she here the whole time. It was clear that as long as she was in the mansion she couldn't trust her five senses, her surroundings, or even the clothes she was wearing, but she had to try.

The bedroom looked very similar to the hallway. There were cracks and holes in the walls and only one dim lit light. The bed looked like someone made it up a long time ago, but now the sheets were much deteriorated. The dressers in the room looked ready to fall apart at a single touch, as the wood they were made of was rotted and splitting.

"There has to be something here I can use!" said Kimberly as she searched in the dressers for any clue or weapon she could use.

While searching she looked over at the closed bedroom door expecting someone or something to break it down at any moment. Her search turned up nothing. She then looked over at the other side of the bed. There was a small table by the bed with a piece of paper and a doll on it. The doll looked homemade. Its main body appeared to be made out of socks. It had green and yellow buttons for eyes. Its hair was in two pigtails and made out of thick black yarn. The dress it was wearing was made out of jeans. Kimberly went over to the table and picked up the paper. She was about to read the piece of paper.

"You'll end up like me, if you don't get out!" said a female voice laughing.

Kimberly's eyes went wide as those were the same words on the paper. She looked down at the doll. The doll was spinning and dancing around the table.

"Yea, just like me, me, me, ME!" laughed the doll.

"I'm so SICK OF THIS SHIT!" yelled Kimberly in a fit of anger as she hit the doll.

The doll hit up against the wall and fell to the floor lifelessly. As it touched the floor barking was heard. Kimberly looked at the window just in time to see the black smoked covered dog crashing through it sending shards of glass all over the room. It landed on the floor letting out a fearsome bark.

"FUCK!" yelled Kimberly as she ran for the door and opened it.

Kimberly ran as fast as she could down the mansion's hallway. She could hear the sounds of the dog's paws heavily pressing against the floor making it greatly creak as it chased her. Kimberly turned the corner in the hallway and saw a staircase leading to the third floor. Unlike the last staircase this one had a doorway in front of it. She ran into the staircase area and closed the door just as the dog ran into it. As a result a huge crack went up the door.

"Crap, that won't hold him for long." said Kimberly as she locked the door and ran up the steps.

Chapter 3

Kimberly ran up the steps as the dog continuously rammed the closed door. Once she stepped foot onto the third floor, a strong wind blew up from under her as if she was running on top of a huge floor air vent.

"I can't move!" thought Kimberly as she felt the air wrap around her, pausing her in the middle of her run.

It all happened in less that a second. Her tennis shoes appeared to be turning back into high heels. At the same time it felt as if the wind was eating away at her pants as they dissolved from the legs up. The high heels as if replacing the pants expanded up her legs becoming high heel boots just stopping a little bit passed her knees. The pants dissolved all the way up to the belt straps but then expanded out becoming a big loincloth with the Velo Nacho logo on it.

Almost as if the air had two strong hands Kimberly felt her arms forcefully moved behind her back. The sleeves of her uniform's jacket were fusing together as if becoming a straight jacket holding her arms in place. The front part of the jacket dissolved away exposing her breast and stomach. The cap she was wearing was melting down on her head. It looked as if it was morphing into a pair of headphones, but instead of small speakers by her ears, long metal plates by her eyes formed instead. They were blinders, the same that are put on a horse to keep it looking straight ahead.

A rod formed between the two blinders and moved up against Kimberly's mouth forcing her to bite into it. She felt two straps wrap around over her shoulders and something heavy clamped down onto her arms behind her back.

WHAP!

"MMMMFFF" said Kimberly as she tried to yell but it was greatly muffed by the mouthpiece.

The sharp pain she felt in her back released her from the pause. She then saw the area change in front of her. It was as if invisible water splashed the mansion hallway washing it away like chalk on a board revealing a huge meadow.

"STOP! I CAN'T STOP!" thought Kimberly as her body was running down the meadow's dirt road against her will.

WHAP! The item that caused the sharp pain hit Kimberly in her back once more.

"Faster, Pepper! Let's show them that you're the fastest delivery pony girl in town." said Bill as he held the straps attached to Kimberly in one hand and a whip in the other hand.

Kimberly was wearing an erotic pony girl costume and was pulling a small carriage that Bill was sitting in. There was a metal rod that came from the base of the carriage and it hooked onto the back of Kimberly's pony girl straight jacket. Bill used the straps to help guide Kimberly in the direction he wanted her to go. The more he whipped her the faster she ran.

"STOP! STOP! SSTTOOPP!" Kimberly yelled mentally.

Kimberly wanted to cry but her body wouldn't let her. After about five minutes of running they came upon a group of farmers working in the fields. Soon a big red barn was in Kimberly's sights.

"Halt!" yelled Bill as he pulled on the straps.

Kimberly started slowing down and stopped about ten feet from the barn. Bill got off the carriage with a few pizza boxes and walked up to the barn. Kimberly just stood where she was not moving. She was mentally yelling as a farmer walked up to her.

"You're really sweaty." said a farmer as he used a towel to wipe her face dry.

"What the… You darn pervert!" thought Kimberly as the farmer used the towel to dry the sweat off her exposed breast and stomach.

"Don't be so rude. The fun is just starting." said the farmer as his voice changed and he walked away out of her field of vision.

Kimberly was shocked and her face expression would have showed it as well if she could move. Not only did it appear that he read her thoughts but his voice changed sounding just like Roland. However that farmer looked nothing like him. Thoughts of worry filled her mind even more then before. She was then startled as she felt the carriage rock back and forth.

WHAP!

"Come on! Pepper we have another delivery to make!" said Bill as he was now on the carriage cracking his whip at her.

Kimberly's body started running on its own again as Bill used the straps to make her turn the carriage around. It just a few short minutes of running Kimberly saw a bridge up ahead. As she was getting closer to it she noticed that the bridge was broken leading to a forty foot drop down to the water below. However Bill continued leading Kimberly towards it.

"Faster, Pepper, faster!" yelled Bill.

"Bill, ARE YOU BLIND! MAKE ME STOP, PLEASE!" yelled Kimberly mentally as her feet touched the bridge.

Suddenly Kimberly saw the area wash over again transforming back into the mansion's third floor hallway. A stone pillar appeared in the hallway right in front of Kimberly as she ran right into it face first. As she fell to the hallway floor she felt the heavy weight of the carriage vanish.

"OWWW!" yelled Kimberly as she rolled on the floor with her hands over her face.

She stopped rolling as she realized she was moving of her own free will. She sat up and saw that she was once again in her pizza delivery uniform. There was no sign of the carriage or Bill, but the familiar sound of the dog ramming the other side of the door that led to the third floor's steps filled the area.

"Crap, whoever is behind all of this is treating me like their personal toy. I have to find a way out of here." said Kimberly.

Kimberly saw two huge double doors down the hallway. She quickly, but cautiously walked towards them. Bracing herself she entered into the room. She expected another area change but instead she heard a clicking sound. The double doors had locked behind her.

"Shit!" said Kimberly as she tried opening the doors.

Banging noises were then heard coming from the far side of the room. She turned around giving the room her full attention. She was in the mansion's kitchen. It was a huge room with many tables, stoves and other kitchen appliances. This room didn't look as rundown as the hallway, but there were cracks in the walls and rusted pots everywhere. A tall and very fat man wearing a chef uniform came out from the upper part of the kitchen holding various cooking ingredients. He sat them down on a counter next to a stove and then reached into a cabinet pulling out a big pot. Kimberly stood there watching him waiting for him to attack her, but he continued setting up to cook as if she wasn't there.

"You're not fooling me." thought Kimberly.

She saw a mop by the door and unscrewed the metal stick from it. The end of the stick was brittle. She hit that end against a table giving the end a jagged edge. She looked back at the chef. He was still ignoring her putting his ingredients into the pot. She slowly walked towards him ready to swing the metal stick at any moment. As she passed by some of the tables she saw a pizza box on one of them. It was the same pizza box she gave Mr. Rowich, the receipt sticker on the box showed his order. It started shaking as if something was trapped inside.

"Oh no you don't!" said Kimberly as she lunges the stick forward to stab the box.

At lighting speed the pizza box opened and a life size adult human arm made of cheese came out rising from the pizza inside. Its hand caught the stick.

"Yeow!" yelled Kimberly as the arm from the box forcefully yanked the stick from her causing her to fall.

"Foolish woman!" yelled a female voice.

The hand threw the metal stick across the room. Kimberly quickly got to her feet as she heard bubbling sounds come from the box. A huge basketball sized lump of cheese and pizza toppings with the arm leaped from the box onto the floor. It starts reshaping at a rapid pace into a humanoid form. Kimberly tries to kick it only to be countered by its own kick forcing her to hit up against the wall.

"That's pay back for earlier." said the cheese creature.

Quickly shaking off the pain from hitting the wall Kimberly looked at the cheese creature. It was now in the form of a tall adult woman with her long hair in two pigtails that was all made of cheese. Various pizza toppings like pepperoni, sausage, ham, and mushrooms were all over her body.

"Your appearance is very amusing. So tell me what is going to happen now?" asked Kimberly as she took on a defensive fighting stance.

"Over confident now, are you? You wanted to cry your eyes out a few minutes ago. If I didn't stop that last scene, they would have had you." said the cheese woman.

"So you're saying that you want to help me. As if I would believe a talking pile of PIZZA!" yelled Kimberly as she charged toward the cheese woman with a punch.

The cheese woman sidestepped Kimberly and then kneed her in her stomach. Kimberly was stunned and stumbled backwards. Before Kimberly could recover the cheese woman spin kicked her in the face sending her slamming against one of the kitchen's windows. The force of the impact forced the window's side shutters open and Kimberly was hanging partly out of it.

"Shit, she may look like it, but she isn't made of pizza." thought Kimberly as she tried to get up.

"You really had to do this the hard way." said the cheese woman as she put her hands around Kimberly's neck.

The cheese woman was putting pressure down on Kimberly's neck while trying to force her out the window. Kimberly was struggling to stay inside the room. Her right arm was pinned down between the window and the cheese woman. She was doing all she could to attack the cheese woman with her left arm but it was like she was hitting stone.

"Nice try, but I can make any part of my body as hard as I want. Throwing you out this window should... HEY!" yelled the cheese woman as she felt her pigtails being pulled.

The chef yanked hard on her pigtails. The cheese woman let go of Kimberly's neck as the pulling of her hair caused her to fall. Kimberly slumped to the floor catching her breath. The chef continued pulling on her pigtails dragging her to a nearby table.

"LET ME GO! LET ME GO!" yelled the cheese woman.

"Crap, I need to get a weapon! There!" said Kimberly as she stood up wobbling.

Kimberly saw the metal stick next to one of the kitchen stoves and ran for it. Meanwhile the cheese woman ripped off one of her pigtails and was struggling to stand up as well. The chef was still pulling on the other pigtail trying to drag her back down.

"I won't let you do this!" yelled the cheese woman as she tried to kick him.

The chef grabbed her foot with his hand. He squeezed down on the foot making a hand imprint into it. Using her leg as leverage the chef swung the cheese woman downward making her fall to the floor. He then ripped off her leg as easy as anyone would rip a mozzarella stick. Kimberly picked up the metal stick and looked over at them. The chef was now holding the cheese woman's head against the edge of a table with his left hand. He was also holding a butcher knife in his right hand.

"Shit, if I don't do something I may be next!" thought Kimberly.

"You're not getting me, I will be ba…URK!" yelled the cheese woman as he slammed the knife into the side of her neck.

He held her head against the direction he was cutting and then forced the knife through to the other end cutting off her head. Her headless body fell to the floor while cheese sauce started pouring out of her neck. The chef then felt something stab him. He looked down to see the metal stick coming out of his chest.

"Got you, you son of bitch!" said Kimberly as she was behind him forcing the stick into him more.

The chef quickly turned around forcing her to let go of the stick. Before Kimberly could react he grabbed her by her neck and lifted her into the air. His wound was bleeding badly but it was as if he wasn't affected by it. Kimberly tried reaching for the stick. However he threw her like she was a baseball and she hit up against the kitchen double doors. This forced the doors open and Kimberly fell back out into the hallway.

Chapter 4

"Crap I was treated like some rag doll in there. Fighting those things normally isn't the answer." said Kimberly as she sat up in the hallway.

Kimberly felt pain throughout her whole body. The pain that was in her legs from running around when she was forced to be a pony girl. The pressure of the pain on Kimberly's back as she was thrown against various walls in the kitchen. Kimberly was surprised that she was still in one piece.

"Whoa did someone turn the heat on?" thought Kimberly as she stood up feeling warm air.

Suddenly the walls started to rumble, but the floor felt fine. The double doors to the kitchen vanished away showing just more of the wall as if the kitchen was never there. The sheetrock of the walls was falling apart showing the inner construction of it. The inner construction turned from wood to metal and the metal was heating up turning red.

"I'm not sticking around for this!" said Kimberly as she ran down the hallway.

She ran down the hallway and turned around the corner only to see more doors vanish and the sheetrock completely crumbling from the wall. The heat from the red hot metal was now making Kimberly really sweat. Kimberly was now finding it a little hard to run. Something on the floor was greatly sticking to her feet. Her eyes went wide as she looked down and saw the floor itself was like one huge long pizza.

"This whole hallway… It's like a giant oven!" panicked Kimberly.

There was one door up ahead and Kimberly watched as it changed shape looking like a huge oven door from the inside. Kimberly knew she only had one choice. She had to ram the door open. She covered her face with her arms to protect it from being burned. She successfully rammed the door open but felt that she lost her footing as she ran a few steps into this new room and fell.

"OOOOWWW!" yelled Kimberly as she was in another staircase area and was now tumbling down many steps.

After about ten seconds she hit the floor at the bottom of the staircase. She sat up holding her head as the fall gave her a headache. Looking over herself she didn't see any serious injuries from the fall. The area didn't feel hot anymore either but very cool now. She looked around at the new hallway she was in. It looked normal. All the chandeliers were full with bright lights. The walls were clean with paintings hung on them. As Kimberly stood up she saw a sign that read "1st Floor" on the wall next to the stairs.

"This is the first floor. Great I'm almost out of here!" said Kimberly.

"No you're not!" yelled a familiar voice.

From behind Roland grabbed her arm. Roland was back to his normal size and his clothing was no longer ripped. He swung her back against the wall. He then quickly clamped his hands down on both her arms.

"How dare you, how dare you, leave me!" yelled Roland.

Kimberly didn't speak a word of response. She just stared at him with an annoyed expression on her face.

"SPEAK BITCH!" yelled Roland as he applied pressure to her arms.

As he squeezed her arms Kimberly felt the pain. Kimberly groaned and grinded her teeth as she tried not to yell from the pain.

"Ya know, I enjoyed showing myself off on stage, but I have my limits. I left your strip club because you wanted me to start kissing and sexually dancing with other women on stage." said Kimberly coldly as she tried to ignore the pain.

"I DIDN'T ASK FOR DEFIANCE, WOMAN! BEG FOR FORGIVENESS! BEG TO COME BACK TO ME!" yelled Roland as he applied even more pressure then before.

The pressure he was putting on her made her feel as if she would crumble apart at any moment. Her legs were feeling wobbly again. She knew she would be falling on her knees shortly. She didn't want that to happen. With as much strength as she could she swung her leg upward.

"ARRRGHH!" yelled Roland as he let her go and stumbled back from being kneed in his crotch.

"Drop the act, you're not Roland. He may be a jerk, but he doesn't attack women. Just what the hell are you?!" demanded Kimberly.

Roland had stumbled back against the wall across from Kimberly. He looked up at her with a dead stare and lunges himself toward her. He throws out his left fist for a punch. His left arm busted out of its sleeve as it and his left fist mutated once again to three times its normal size. Before Kimberly could even brace herself for the attack she sees a cloud of smoke instantly appear beside Roland.

A paw with sharp claws comes out of the smoke and digs along the side of Roland's face leaving a deep claw mark. The force of the attack stops Roland as he was less then an inch away from hitting Kimberly. She watches as Roland falls. Roland's head explodes on impact with the floor. Pizza sauce and tomato chunks instead of blood and flesh spatter over the hallway from the impact. Some of it even gets on Kimberly. Her legs finally gave out and she drops to her knees.

She looks over at Roland's body and sees the smoke covered dog licking the pizza sauce on the floor near him. She wanted to run but her legs were too sore. The dog looked at her. ARF! It wasn't aggressive barking. The dog was yapping happily and continued licking up the sauce. Suddenly Kimberly felt a hand come down and rest on her shoulder.

Startled she quickly turns around as fast as she could.

"Calm down, you're safe for now." said a woman in a black and white maid uniform.

The maid was standing in a doorway that wasn't there before. It was at the spot where Roland had her pinned against the wall. The maid was a tall Japanese woman with purple eyes who looked to be in her twenties. She had her long black hair in two pigtails. The black smoke covered dog ran over to the maid. She picked him up. As she did the smoke faded away from him. Kimberly was expecting to see some evil demon bulldog, but to Kimberly's surprise the dog was just a small normal Chihuahua.

"Follow me and hurry. He may recover any minute." said the maid as she turned around and walked into the room.

Hearing that warning, Kimberly got up on her sore legs and walked into the room. She now found herself in a rather large living room. Looking behind her, as she expected, the doorway vanished leaving a wall behind. She quickly sat down on a nearby couch. Looking at the maid again Kimberly shockingly realized something.

"Your hair, the doll, that cheese thing, it was you! How are you alive? You're head was chopped off!" said Kimberly.

"That wasn't me. It was the image of a pizza in your thoughts that I took control off." said the maid.

As if she didn't hear the maid's response Kimberly became very tense. Her legs were too sore to run and she could barely walk. Kimberly was bracing herself for any kind of attack, she had to defend herself. The maid watched as Kimberly balled her fist.

"Sigh… I'm not going to attack you and yes, I'm very sorry about before. My name is Akari Watanabi. I'm here to help you. I will explain all that I know, but it may sound unbelievable to you." said an annoyed Akari as she stood at least ten feet from Kimberly.

"Fine I'll listen, but don't try anything." said a still tense Kimberly.

"Very well, this may be hard to accept, it was for me at first too. The best way I can say it is we're trapped in someone's psychic wave." said Akari.

"What!" said Kimberly as it sounded very absurd.

"To put it simpler, it's like we're trapped in a game. It is unknown who or what makes the waves, but they can control everything in it. It is a battle of willpower, and if they overpower you, they can do almost anything they want, as you have seen. So you must fight back with your own willpower." said Akari.

Kimberly didn't know what to really say. She had been physically attacked and had to fight for her life. Too many weird events had happened including the loss of control over her body. She wanted to know what was going on, but Akari's explanation sounded too far fetched. However it fit with what had been going on, so Kimberly had to ask...

"But how do I fight them?" asked Kimberly.

"Use your imagination of course to manifest things. Think of it this way, you're in a game that anyone can join in at anytime. The wave controller is the game's host. To end the game the host or another player can kick you out. Likewise you can defeat the host. Think of it as being disconnected during a phone call. That's what I tried to do to you earlier." said Akari.

"So you tried to help me by throwing me out a window!" asked Kimberly rudely as she still didn't trust her.

"Yes, a moment of intense shock can knock you off the wave. Now, your current problem, you have to be able to focus on yourself otherwise you will not survive here. Try to picture yourself healed believe that you are healed." said Akari.

Kimberly decided to give it a try. She closed her eyes and filled her mind with thoughts of her body perfectly healed. Within seconds she felt her pain going away. After about fifteen seconds she opened her eyes and looked over herself. Kimberly was fully healed.

"It worked." said Kimberly as she got up and moved around a bit.

"Of course it did, but you'll have to be able to do it instantly, if you are to stand a chance as this may not be the only wave you encounter." said Akari.

"Hold on, now that you mention it, why are we still here? Didn't you defeat the host?" asked Kimberly.

"Yes, the main psychic wave vanished with him, but it left a minor one between us. Once we separate into different locations we'll both be freed from the game we're in." said Akari as she walked toward a new door that appeared in the wall.

"You sound like some cheap game guide more then a player. If is this a game, how can I be sure you're not apart of it?" demanded Kimberly.

"You still don't trust me. Very well, as a guide, I will give you one last piece of advice, don't ever lose, never. If you are going to lose, retreat instead. If you lose the host can change you outside the game. It's already started to happen because the host almost beat you." said Akari as she opened the door and stood in the doorway.

"Wait! You just can't leave after saying that! What's going to happen to me?" yelled a worried Kimberly as she quickly walked toward Akari.

Before Kimberly could reach her, Akari walked out the door and closed it behind her. By the time Kimberly touched the door it was already partly faded away. Kimberly stood there for about a minute after the door was gone. Nothing was happening.

"Why am I still here? Maybe if I leave this room." said Kimberly.

Kimberly looked around the huge living room there were no doors or exits of any kind.

"No, no, no! She said this would be over once we separated. Why am I STILL HERE!" yelled Kimberly.

"Simple it's not over yet. I'm the real host. " said an unknown male voice, as if it was coming from an intercom.

"I've had enough of this crap! Just show yourself." yelled Kimberly.

"Hmm, guess I'll get right to the point then. That loud mouth woman you were talking to didn't have all the facts right. However, for what they are, doesn't matter now." said the voice.

Suddenly all the furniture vanished away, even the living room's carpet disappeared showing the wooden floor underneath. The paint on the walls faded away showing the true dim gray color of the sheetrock walls. The living room was now completely bare.

"Time to start over I'm going to train you from the ground up." said the voice as it changed in sound from a male voice to a female voice.

The voice had sounded clearer this time as if the person talking was right behind her. Kimberly quickly turned around as she realized this particular female voice all too well. The sight of the woman shocked Kimberly and she cautiously took a few steps back. The woman was her, another Kimberly.

Chapter 5

Kimberly stood at least ten feet from her double. There was a stark contrast between them. Kimberly was wearing her blue and purple Velo Nacho uniform while her double was wearing the dark blue leather lingerie. Kimberly hated the look of the double's posture. The mischievous way she stood and walked with her hands on her hips while slightly leaning back and forth to show off her body's curves. That was the same routine Kimberly did at the club as Pepper to attract men. However, now as unpleasant as it seemed Pepper was the one standing across from Kimberly.

"I'm not amused! Just who are you?" demanded Kimberly as she went into an offensive fighting stance.

"My, my, what you should be asking is why you took that stupid pizza job. The money that job pays in a week you could make at the club in one night. If only you stayed there. All you had to do was show off some more of your extra TALENTS." laughed Pepper.

That remark made Kimberly very frustrated. She balled her fist and grinded her teeth.

"All you had to do was perform some GROUP activities on stage and even some backstage wouldn't have hurt either." smirked Pepper.

"Shut up!" yelled Kimberly.

Kimberly, in a rage, ran toward Pepper preparing to grab her neck. However Kimberly's hands suddenly came into contact with something. She stopped herself before her body fully hit up against it. Quickly inspecting the area, there appeared to be an invisible wall between Kimberly and Pepper.

"Coward!" yelled Kimberly as she slammed her fist against the wall.

"Coward... that is what I want changed! Just as this room needs a makeover, so do you! I'm sick of you holding me back!" said Pepper.

"What the hell are you talking about?!" demanded Kimberly.

"I'm YOU and yet all the opportunities I missed are because of you, that stupid moral code of yours. I could have had them all in my hands!" yelled Pepper.

"Stop with the stupid mind games! I worked only as a stripper not a whore! I won't degrade myself to that level!" yelled Kimberly as she tried attacking the wall again.

"You don't have the resolve to break that wall. You can't reach me." said Pepper as she waved her right hand downward.

Suddenly two men appeared tied up beside Pepper.

"What the... What are you going to do!" yelled Kimberly as she realized who the two men were.

The two men are Roland and Bill. They are both on their knees only wearing shorts. Their legs are tied up and their hands are tied behind their backs. They are also blindfolded and had ball gags in their mouths. A blue leather whip appears in Pepper's left hand.

"Roland is a real wimp. He's been calling your phone and leaving messages begging you to come back to the club since you left and yet you refuse to answer him." said Pepper as she rubbed the top of Roland's head with her right hand.

"How do you..." said Kimberly, but she was interrupted by Pepper's sneering laugh.

"HOW DO I KNOW ABOUT IT? I'M YOU!" laughed Pepper as she swung her right hand downward while pulling on Roland's hair.

Pepper let go of Roland and his head hit the floor with a loud thud sound. Pepper snapped her whip and begun hitting Roland's back with it. Kimberly helplessly watched as long red bruise marks appeared on Roland's back with each hit.

"See how easy it is! SEE! You could have had your way with him easily!" said Pepper as she hit Roland with the whip for the eleventh time.

"I'm not a whore! Stop with the stupid show!" yelled Kimberly.

"Hmm…" said Pepper as she appeared to be ignoring Kimberly while using her right heel to nudge the back of Roland's head.

"He passed out, oh well on to the next one." said Pepper as she walked toward Bill.

"STOP!" yelled Kimberly as she hit the wall again and this time it caused a small flash on impact with the wall.

Kimberly hit the wall several more times as rapidly as she could. The small flashes soon stopped appearing as they were replaced by a shine on the wall. The wall was now visible. It was a thick clear glass wall and there was a small crack in the area where Kimberly had been hitting.

"Oh… Well you won't get any farther then that." said Pepper as she started to reach out to grab Bill.

"SSTTTOOOPP!!" yelled Kimberly as she hit the wall once more but the crack didn't get any larger.

"Stop, why would I stop something you want to do? Bill is a regular customer at the club. Since he has seen you naked on stage you've been wondering why he hasn't made a pass at you yet." said Pepper.

"SHUT UP YOU DON'T KNOW NOTH…" yelled Kimberly as she was once again cut off by Pepper's laughter.

Without warning the room started to spin wildly and the sound of Pepper's laughter faded away. The room became one big blur, Kimberly couldn't recognize anything. She closed her eyes to avoid getting dizzy.

"This is another trick, I won't get caught!" said Kimberly as she went back into her offensive fighting stance ready to strike anything that came near her.

Suddenly Kimberly felt her left hand grab something out of midair. It was as if her hand had a mind of its own. She tried to make her left hand drop the item, but her left hand didn't respond as it continued to grip the item tightly. Finally more worried about her hand then the room she opened her eyes. The room was no longer spinning, but…

"NO WAY!" panicked Kimberly as she was holding Pepper's whip in her left hand.

Looking down past the whip Kimberly saw that Bill was beside her. Kimberly and Pepper had switched places. She then noticed that the left sleeve of her Velo Nacho jacket was gone. She quickly looked over herself and then looked at Pepper. They were both wearing the dark blue leather lingerie. The only part of the Velo Nacho uniform left on Kimberly was just the cap on her head.

"Like I said I won't stop something you want to do. WHIP HIM!" ordered Pepper.

"No! I won't do it!" yelled Kimberly as she still tried to let go of the whip, but her left hand held it firmly.

Kimberly's left hand begun to shake as if it was trying to guide her left arm to swing the whip. Kimberly quickly held her left hand down with her right hand. Seeing this whole scene made Kimberly think of just how could she have gotten like this.

When Kimberly worked at the Ten Pleasures Strip club she was one of the most requested strippers to be on stage, but she was also one of the few moral women there that wasn't a prostitute. The contrast of the two made working in that environment a bit awkward for her because men often offered to pay her for sexual favors. However she refused them all. This may have been the reason why they got tired of her stage act.

Bill was different, he never asked for sexual favors. He enjoyed her performance and tipped big when he could. He had a certain honest charm that she couldn't help but like. Until the time she left the club, seeing him was one of her reasons for being there.

"Wait, that's it, isn't it?" thought Kimberly as she broke out her daze.

Kimberly's left hand finally opened up and dropped the whip.

"Everything appears to be fine." said Kimberly as she inspected her left hand while moving her fingers back and forth.

"No, how could you have gotten free?" said Pepper as she rushed up to her side of the glass wall.

"Forget it, I'm not going back to the club." said Kimberly.

"You know you want to go back, the money…" yelled Pepper.

"Money isn't worth my dignity. Going back there will only mean I'll submit to what they want." said Kimberly as she interrupted Pepper.

"So what, give them their fantasies while draining all of them dry to get what you want." yelled Pepper.

"No, I will get by with what I earn from a more honest living and currently the place for that is here." said Kimberly as she adjusted her Velo Nacho cap.

Suddenly the rest of Kimberly's Velo Nacho uniform appeared on her.

"FOOL! You could achieve your goals and dreams faster by..." raged Pepper.

"BY WHAT, BEING A WHORE, HAVING TO DEAL WITH CONSEQUENCES THAT WILL DESTORY MY GOALS AND RUIN MY LIFE!" yelled Kimberly as she interrupted Pepper again and kicked the glass wall.

A new crack formed in the wall from where she had kicked. It was much larger then the crack her earlier punch made. The crack quickly spread over about 2/3 of the glass wall looking like the pattern of some wild growing tree.

"NO! YOU CAN'T DO THIS!" yelled Pepper.

With all her might Kimberly kicked the glass wall once more. The wall shattered into a million pieces. Pepper shattered as well as if she had been nothing more then Kimberly's reflection on the glass wall.

Finally tired of it all Kimberly sat down on the floor in between Roland and Bill. She couldn't stand the sight of Roland as it was a reminder of that night. When they couldn't get Kimberly to whore herself out, they tried to get her to perform like a whore instead of a dancer on stage. Kimberly rose up her fist as she prepared to punch Roland's head. Suddenly a hand came down on her shoulder as she was about to strike.

"Kimberly, wake up!" said a voice.

The echo of the voice went all over the room repeating. Kimberly turned around to look behind her, but as she did the whole area faded into darkness. The voice got louder as it continued repeating. Suddenly a dim light appeared a few feet in front of Kimberly and caused her to open her eyes.

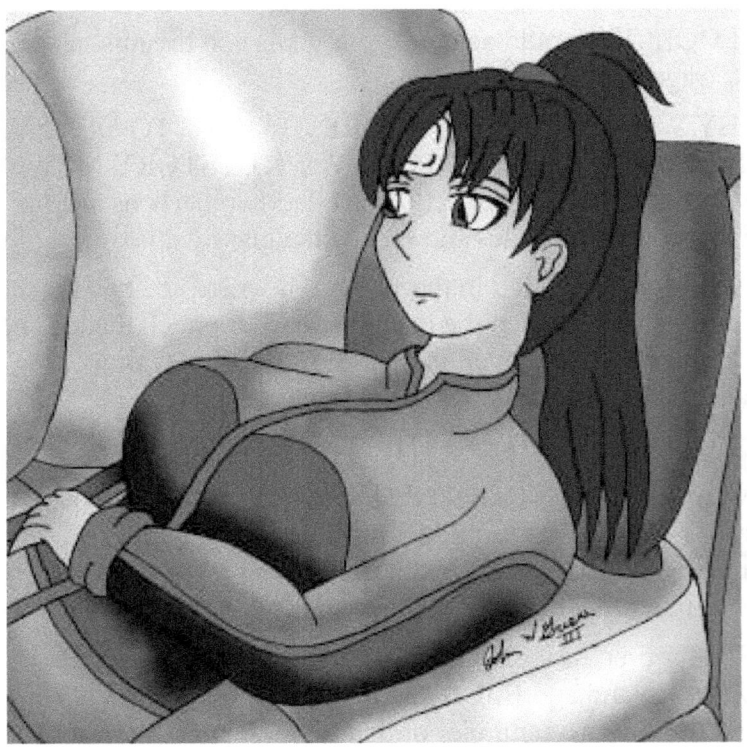

"Bill…" said Kimberly, as she sat up.

Kimberly saw that she had been lying on a couch in a living room. Bill was beside her, kneeling down next to the couch. He was wearing his Velo Nacho manager's uniform. She felt a brief headache come over her as she sat up and put her hand on her forehead only to feel a small bandage on it.

"Don't touch it. The doctor called me when he bought you inside and treated the wound. I was afraid that you had gone into a coma or something." said Bill.

"Doctor?" asked Kimberly.

"Yeah that was a real scare you gave me. When I opened the door to get my pizza you passed out and hit your head on my steps. It's just a small scar but more then that you appear to have passed out from some minor food poisoning. " said Mr. Rowich as he walked into the room.

"That can't be. All the ingredients my pizza shop uses are all fresh." said Bill.

"I suggest that you double check it all and the people who work with it. Miss what did you eat today?" asked Mr. Rowich.

"Well aside from the medium pizza I had for lunch. I had one of the shop's new pizza sticks. Bill it had way too much of a spicy taste." said Kimberly.

"That shouldn't be, I don't use a lot of spices in my recipe. I will check on it first thing tomorrow. The shop had just closed for the night." said Bill.

"Very well, in any case it's just minor food poisoning she'll be fine by tomorrow. Just give her the day off tomorrow." said Mr. Rowich.

Kimberly rested her head against one of the couch's soft cushions. She wasn't sure if she should tell them of the weird adventure she had. It seemed way too real to just be a dream, but at least the worst appeared to be over.

"Kimberly, sorry about this, I'll give you the day off with pay." said Bill as he stood up and two cardboard objects fell from his pocket onto the floor.

"What's this, movie tickets?" said Kimberly as she picked them up.

"Well I was going to ask tomorrow if you wanted to go out in the evening to celebrate your new job. The movie was just one of the things I had planned. Guess its bad timing to ask now." said Bill.

"No it's not, I accept. So what else did you have planned?" said Kimberly with a smile.

"If I told you it wouldn't be a surprise now would it?" asked a happy Bill.

"She should rest for tonight. That couch folds out into a bed, feel free to stay until morning. I have to finish some paperwork, if you need anything just call." said Mr. Rowich.

"Thanks." said Bill.

Mr. Rowich nodded and left the room.

"Bill, I've been meaning to ask, why is the name of the pizza shop, Velo Nacho?" asked Kimberly.

"There is an interesting story behind that. You see Velo is short for velocity and Nacho is a type of chip. So the name can be broken down to, Fast Chips. The funny thing is how the name was picked out." said Bill as he chatted away.

The conversation continued as Kimberly and Bill begin to chat about various things. It ranged from subjects like personal experience, happy moments, and views on life. She was finally getting to know Bill more and more.

Epilogue

Three Months Later…

Kimberly was no longer a delivery woman for Velo Nacho instead she was working as the cashier during the pizza shop's daytime hours. She now viewed the strange events at Rowich's mansion as some introverted dream. A dream about how undecided she was at the time of the choices: money or dignity. Indeed Roland and Pepper played the part of her that wanted to be back on stage no matter what, but Kimberly realized she had to let it go and she's glad she did.

However there was one thing that didn't fit in the dream. The woman named Akari Watanabi had nothing to do with Kimberly's situation. Akari was trying to explain the dream as if it was some type of video game. Kimberly viewed Akari as just the manifestation of the fact that she liked video games. That changed when she heard that a stripper with that same name went missing almost a year ago. Kimberly soon just considered it to be a coincidence.

Ever since that day Bill always double checked for any tainted food. The day he had checked for the spices, everything turned out to be in good condition. The four chefs on duty that day also denied using extra spices in the pizza sticks. A week afterward one of the chefs left for another job.

Kimberly's relationship with her boyfriend Bill was going great. She was happy to hear he no longer had a reason to go to the club after all he now had her. Kimberly had cut all ties with the club except for a few friends that worked there. From them she was told something unexpected, apparently Mr. Rowich had bought the Ten Pleasures Strip club.

2:14am on the night Kimberly and Bill stayed at Rowich's mansion…

Mr. Rowich was in his office on the third floor, he was talking with someone on the phone.

"They are asleep at the moment. They don't suspect anything and think it's just minor food poisoning. Have the targets left town already?" said Mr. Rowich.

"Yes, the targets have left. If I just didn't put that stuff in the wrong order. What were you going to make those business officials hallucinate about anyway?" said the chef.

"Hallucinate, is an understatement. Once 'it' is ingested the victim's brain becomes more sensitive to telepathy and other forms of mental psychic attacks. A psychic could easily read the victim's mind like an open book and even rewrite their very personality if their mind is weak enough." said Mr. Rowich.

"And what of that delivery woman?" asked the chef.

"A waste of time mostly, she is a little strong willed. If that bothersome Akari didn't show up I could have had her. She is of no importance, but we must deal with Akari as soon as possible. I did however learn something of interest." said Mr. Rowich.

"Just what might that be?" asked the chef.

"First I'll need you to do something for me. We're about to have a bunch of new test subjects in our hands." said Mr. Rowich slightly laughing.

The Art Gallery

Kimberly's Pepper Reflection

Kimberly Warren in her Velo Nacho uniform

Kimberly Warren in her dark blue leather lingerie

Kimberly runs from the crumbling floor

Kimberly fights for her life against a woman made out of cheese and pizza toppings

Kimberly in an erotic pony girl costume pulling a small carriage

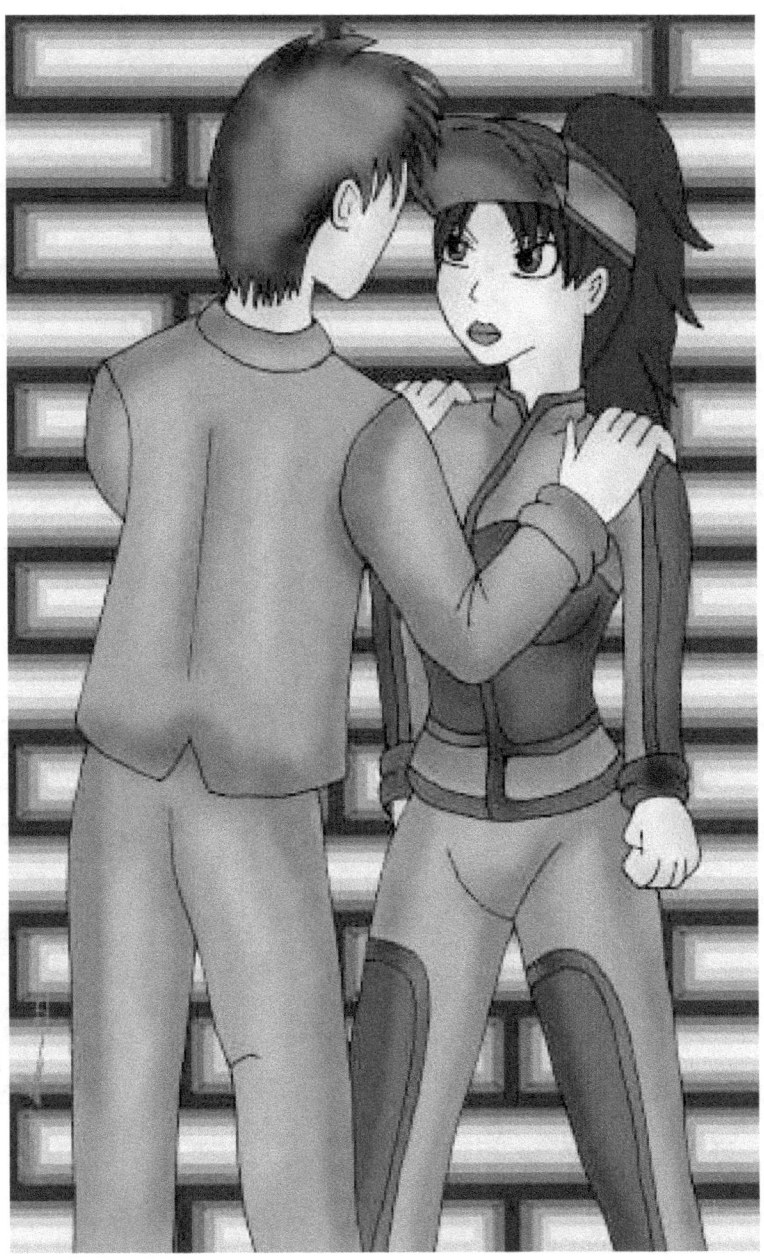

Kimberly's unwanted meeting with Roland

Kimberly finally "wakes up" from her ordeal

Akari Watanabi and her pet Chihuahua

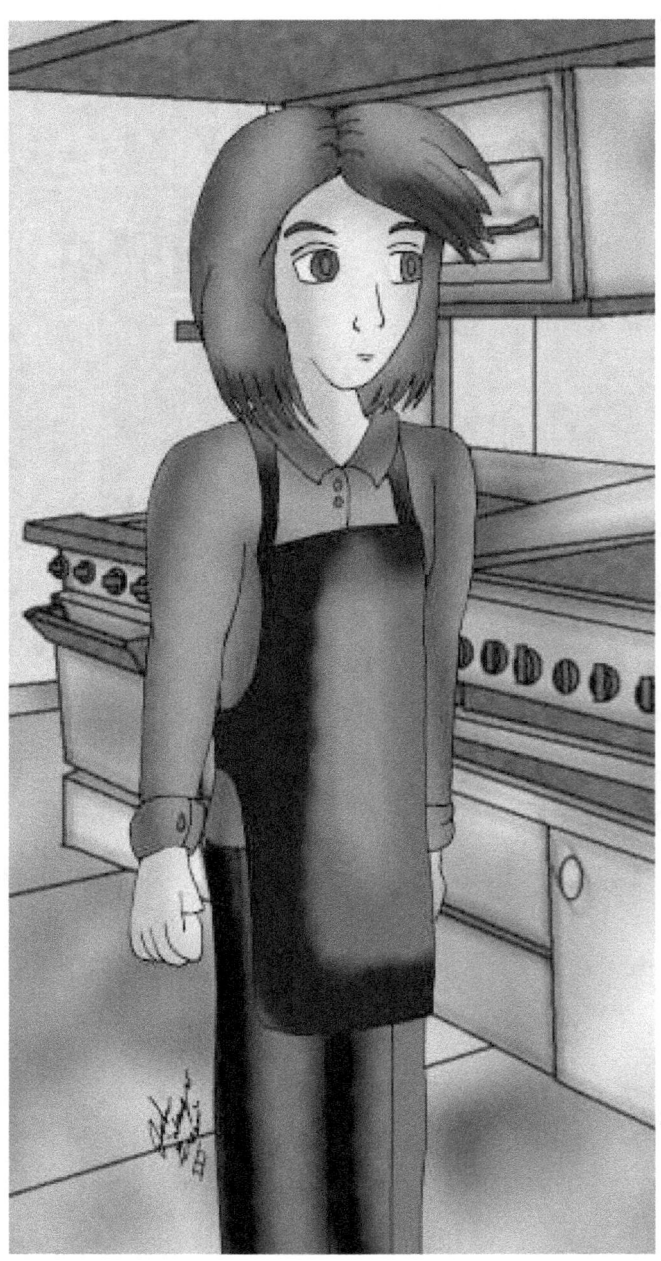

Bill Karson

Roland Dixon

Mr. Rowich

The story will continue in: The Vicwelt Mansion Vol.2